TOMORROW
STARTS TODAY

DISNEY
ANDI·MACK

TOMORROW
STARTS TODAY

Adapted by Elizabeth Rudnick
Based on the series created by Terri Minsky
Part One is based on the episode "13," written by Terri Minsky.
Part Two is based on the episode "Dancing in the Dark," written by Phil Baker.

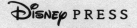

DISNEY PRESS
Los Angeles • New York

Printed in the United States of America
First Paperback Edition, August 2018
1 3 5 7 9 10 8 6 4 2
Library of Congress Control Number: 2018936687
ISBN 978-1-368-02679-6
FAC-029261-18173

For more Disney Press fun, visit www.disneybooks.com
Visit DisneyChannel.com

SUSTAINABLE
FORESTRY
INITIATIVE

Certified Chain of Custody
Promoting Sustainable Forestry

www.sfiprogram.org
SFI-01054

The SFI label applies to the text stock

CHAPTER 1

My mom is going to be so mad at me.

Looking down at the electric scooter's dashboard, Andi hesitated. The keys jingled on the end of her finger as her hand shook. She wasn't sure if she was shaking because she was nervous (after all, she had never ridden a scooter before) or because she was scared (after all, she had never defied her mother before—then again, she had never been almost thirteen before).

Taking a deep breath, she lowered the shiny black helmet over her brown pixie cut. *Be brave, Andi Mack,* she said to herself. *You can do this!* Then, before she could change her mind, Andi put the key in the ignition and turned it. With a loud roar—or rather a very loud purr—the scooter came to life. Gripping the handlebars, Andi took off.

As the scooter raced along the path toward the center of town, Andi tried not to scream. It felt like she was going a million miles an hour. The wind tugged at her jacket, making the white racing stripes flutter, and she was pretty sure that if the helmet hadn't been covering every inch of her face, she would have gotten a serious case of windburn. Narrowly missing a tree, Andi took a corner—a bit faster than she had anticipated—and found herself looking out over a very steep hill.

This time she didn't even attempt to hold back the scream.

"AHHHHHHH!"

Finally, the terrible hill flattened out, and Andi rolled onto Main Street. She clutched the handlebars as she weaved through people and traffic. For a brief moment, Andi felt like she was finally getting the hang of the scooter. *Maybe buying this thing without telling anyone wasn't such a bad idea after all.* But then she rounded a corner and nearly flattened her two best friends before stopping.

"Whoa!" Cyrus shouted, nearly dropping his bright blue water bottle as he jumped back in fear.

"Watch where you're going, psycho!" Buffy said. Unlike Cyrus, Buffy didn't seem scared. She just looked annoyed, or angry, or ready to speak her mind. It was hard to tell. That was one of Buffy's many talents—keeping people guessing.

Behind the opaque mask of her helmet, Andi smiled. Her best friends were so different from each other. Yet somehow, those differences seemed to make their friendship stronger. Cyrus was the sensitive one, always ready to help out and listen. He also happened to be totally tuned in to pop culture and was Andi's go-to person when she was coming up with something new and crafty in her art shack. Buffy, on the other hand, was more a "tough love" kind of friend. She looked all sweetness and light with her big brown eyes and wide smile. But she was strong-minded—and not afraid of confrontation. Like now, for example, as she clenched her hands into fists at her sides.

Catching his breath, Cyrus stepped forward. "You could have killed us!" he shouted. But any further protest died on his lips as Andi finally took off her helmet and her friends realized who had nearly run them over.

"*Andi!*" he and Buffy exclaimed together.

Andi smiled, flipping her bangs out of her face. "Sorry! I haven't figured out the brakes yet," she said. "So . . . what do you think? Do you like it?"

Buffy and Cyrus rushed forward and began examining the shiny yellow scooter. They gushed as they checked out the metal handlebars and the fancy dials on the dashboard. They agreed: they didn't just like the new bike; they *loved* it. But Buffy had one question.

"When do you think you'll take off the training wheels?" she asked, pointing at the back of the bike.

Andi glanced at the two shiny new training wheels that were supporting the back wheel of the scooter. Looking at her friends, she laughed sheepishly. So she wasn't *quite* a total rebel . . . not yet, at least. But the training wheels wouldn't be there forever. The next day Andi was turning thirteen. That meant no more training wheels. And when they came off, there would be no stopping Andi Mack.

Andi turned and began to walk the scooter along Shadyside's one and only Main Street sidewalk. Her friends fell in beside her. "I can't believe your mom let you get this," Cyrus said as they walked. They strolled past the same stores that had been there their whole lives. From the brick-fronted barbershop, with its traditional red, white, and blue post, to the flower shop, displaying dozens of bouquets, Main Street seemed perfect and picturesque.

"Oh, she has no idea," Andi said. Cyrus's tone had been teasing, but he knew as well as she did that her mom was not the easygoing type. She was the opposite. "I traded in my bike. That plus the money I made cat sitting for the Wadmans." It had been hard for her to give up that money—the cat was not easy to sit for—but Andi had done it anyway. She had never bought anything so, well, grown-up with her own money before. While she knew it was probably going to land her in hot water, it still felt good.

And then Buffy rained reality on her parade.

"Hold on. Back up," Buffy said, pulling on the straps of her backpack. "You really think she'll let you keep this thing? The woman who wouldn't let you within ten feet of a bouncy castle?"

Andi nodded. True, her mother was tough. True,

her mother was not a fan of fun. Or adventure. But this was different. "All of that changes as of tomorrow," she said.

Cyrus furrowed his dark eyebrows. "What happens tomorrow?"

"I turn thirteen," Andi reminded her friends. "I become a teenager. It means I get to rebel."

"Yeah, sure," Cyrus agreed. "Do that." Andi's hopes lifted. She had known Cyrus would understand. Then he continued. "But maybe start with something simple? Some black nail polish. Or"—he paused for dramatic effect—"part your hair . . . on the other side." He ran his hands through his own thick dark hair and left it standing straight up.

Andi couldn't help smiling at her friend's take on rebellion. She wasn't really trying to rebel. Honestly, she was just tired of hearing someone say no every time she opened her mouth. She figured that if she didn't ask, then her mom couldn't say no. Wasn't there some expression about doing now and asking for forgiveness later? She was just going to have to ask for forgiveness—a *lot* of forgiveness—*after* her mom saw the scooter.

Unfortunately, that moment was all too quick in coming. Shadyside wasn't a big town, which meant its Main Street wasn't exactly long. And since Andi lived right near Main Street, she and her friends arrived in front of her house way faster than she would have liked.

Stopping, she gazed up at her home. It looked perfect, just the way her mother liked it. The plants that lined the front walkway were impeccably trimmed. Bright flowers hung from flowerpots along the big wrap-around porch, and the gray siding looked as though it had been painted that morning. Nothing was out of place. Andi was pretty sure not even a blade of grass dared to grow in the wrong direction—not under her mother's watchful eye.

The whole way over, she had kept talking about being brave and bold and how being a teenager was going to change her. But now, standing in front of her house, she felt some of that boldness slipping away.

Buffy was quick to notice. "I'm impressed," she said, raising her eyebrows. "We made it almost to your driveway before you chickened out."

"I'm not chickening out," Andi protested. *I'm totally chickening out,* she thought, throwing a desperate look in Cyrus's direction.

Cyrus saw the look and knew instantly what Andi needed. "I can hide it in my garage," he offered.

Andi let out a sigh of relief. She had known Cyrus would come through for her. Thanking him, she turned to hand off the scooter and get inside before her mom saw them standing there. But just as she lifted her fingers from the handlebars, a loud roar came from the end of the street.

The three friends looked toward the sound and watched as a large black motorcycle turned onto Andi's street. Cyrus began to grin. Buffy's eyes grew wide. "Whoa," she said, nudging Andi with her elbow. "Now *that's* the real deal."

"I like yours better," Cyrus said, patting Andi on the shoulder in an attempt to make her feel better.

Andi barely noticed. She knitted her eyebrows as the bike came closer and closer. Then, to her surprise, it turned—into her driveway. The engine gave one last loud roar, and then the bike came to a stop. In the silence that followed, Buffy's and Cyrus's impressed gasps sounded louder than the bike's engine had. "Who is that?" Buffy asked at the same time Cyrus wondered, "Do you know anyone who . . ."

They all watched as the mystery bike rider took off a helmet. This time, it was Andi's turn to gasp. She *did* know someone who rode a motorcycle.

"Bex!" she cried. Dropping her backpack next to the scooter, she raced up the driveway and flung her arms around her big sister.

CHAPTER 2

"Hey, Andiman!"

Andi's arms tightened around her sister as Bex swung her around. Laughing, Andi enjoyed the moment for as long as she could. She hadn't known Bex was coming home. Despite the age difference, Andi and Bex got along great. Whenever her sister was home, Andi felt like things made more sense.

Her parents, on the other hand, weren't always as thrilled by Bex's sudden appearances and disappearances. Her sister was what her mom called a free spirit. While the label was often intended as a compliment, Andi suspected her mom didn't mean it that way. Whatever way it was used, though, Andi knew what it meant. It meant that Bex liked to live life to the fullest. She traveled the world and wasn't afraid to try new things or meet new people. *I doubt she would have been nervous to buy a scooter,* Andi thought as Bex lowered Andi's feet back to the ground. *Come to think of it, now that she's here, I should ask Bex's advice on what to say to Mom. . . .*

Turning, she gestured for Buffy and Cyrus to come over. "Guys!" she said happily. "It's my sister!" As her friends walked up the driveway, Cyrus pushing the scooter, Andi looked back at her sister. While she was happy to have Bex home, she couldn't help asking, "What are you doing here?"

Bex leaned down, resting her hands on her torn jeans. Her hair, wavy and dark, brushed along the shoulders of her leather jacket. It wasn't just the motorcycle; Bex simply radiated cool. From her turquoise-and-black choker to her graphic T-shirt, Bex looked every inch the free spirit. Andi wished, not for the first time, that she had gotten some of her big sister's style and personality.

"What do you mean? I couldn't miss your birthday!" Bex said, answering Andi's question and snapping her back to the moment. Then Bex tilted her head thoughtfully. "Which, don't say it . . . I know I've missed most of them—"

"I don't care!" Andi said, cutting her sister off. "You're here now."

Buffy and Cyrus, who had been waiting for the reunion excitement to die down, stepped forward. Seeing them, Bex smiled. While she might have flitted into and out of Andi's life for the past thirteen years, she had been around enough to get to know her friends—at least her two best friends. "Cyrus," she said as he approached, still holding on to the scooter. Her eyebrows came together as she took in the bright yellow machine. "Are those your wheels?"

Beside her, Andi nodded to Cyrus and mouthed the word yes. She had every intention of getting Bex's advice about the scooter, just not quite yet.

Cyrus picked up on the not-so-subtle hint. "Yeah," he answered, clapping his hands together. "Totally. Full-throttle outlaw." He stopped. He didn't need to see the look on Buffy's face to know that he sounded ridiculous. "Those are all the biker words I know," he said, shrugging.

Lucky for Cyrus, his word vomit of biker lingo didn't

seem to bother or confuse Bex too much. Turning her attention to Andi's other BFF, she smiled warmly. Bex had always had a soft spot for Buffy. "Wow," she said, taking in the girl's fashionable orange jacket and boho blue top. "You're turning into the real Buffy."

"I *am* a real Buffy. And I would prefer not being compared to a fictional vampire slayer on a television show from the last century," she snapped. That was clearly not the first time someone had made the connection. But then she paused and looked a bit sheepish. "Although . . . I recently started watching it and it is pretty good," she admitted with a laugh.

As their laughter died, Andi turned back to Bex. "So, does Mom know you're here?" she asked.

"I wanted it to be a surprise," Bex said, lifting her hands into the air and making a face like she hoped that was a good thing.

Andi frowned. Her mother hated surprises. She hated surprises almost as much as she hated her lawn not being perfect. Or saying yes to anything Andi asked for that wasn't "safe" or "smart." In other words, she really, *really* hated surprises. Quickly, Andi pointed that out to Bex.

"Yeah," Bex said. "Will you come with me?" she asked hopefully. "And tell her?"

Smiling, Andi nodded. Of course she would help. After all, wasn't that what sisters were for?

* * *

Andi burst through the front door of her house and barreled across the living room toward the sounds of someone cooking in the kitchen. Like the outside, the inside of the Macks' home was perfectly put together. Dark wood antique pieces blended seamlessly with more modern touches. Beautiful rugs lay over the hard-wood floors, which did not appear to have a scratch on them—thanks to Andi's mother's cleaning, of course. Pictures drawn by Andi when she was younger lined the wall by the stairs leading up to the second floor. There was at least one framed photo of Andi on every flat surface, from bookshelf to console table . . . and a few of Bex were mixed in for good measure.

In the kitchen, Andi's father, Ham, was busily stir-ring cake batter. A rag was flung over his shoulder in case of any possible mess making, but otherwise he was as spotless as the house around him. His dark hair had only recently started to gray, giving him a salt-and-pepper look. For a man with one grown daughter and an almost teenager, he still looked young, and his eyes, which were bright, brightened even more as Andi and Bex rushed in.

"Dad! Look who came home for my birthday!" Andi said, letting go of her sister's hand so Bex could give her father a hug.

"Bex! What a wonderful surprise!" he said, giving Bex a big squeeze. Hearing footsteps on the stairs, he looked over as his wife walked down. "Celia, look who's here!"

Celia raised an eyebrow as she took in the reunion occurring in the kitchen. "I see," she said flatly. Like the home she worked to keep perfect, Celia was also perfect. Not a strand of hair was out of place, and her silver necklace matched the simple earrings she wore.

"Hi, Mom," Bex said.

"Rebecca," Celia replied, using her daughter's full name to show her displeasure. She gave her daughter a once-over. "You look . . . well," she said, her tone implying otherwise. "How long will you be staying?"

Standing next to her big sister, Andi shifted uncomfortably on her feet. She knew that her mom and Bex didn't have the best of relationships, but she always wished she knew why. It was like there was something between them, some story, that made moments like that feel awkward at best. Right then, it was as though they were strangers meeting at a party, not a mother and daughter who hadn't seen each other in a while.

"Okay," Bex said, picking up on her mother's unwelcoming question, "so much for the pleasantries, huh?" She frowned but kept an arm around Andi. She had known that the surprise visit wasn't going to be her mom's cup of tea. But she was less worried about the surprise and more worried about the news she was about to deliver. Looking at her father, she nodded at Celia. "Dad, can you brace Mom and give her something to grab?"

Andi's father walked over to stand behind his wife and put his hands on her shoulders. Together, the pair waited to hear what Bex had to say.

"I'll be staying a while," she said, her voice rising at the end of the statement involuntarily. She hadn't meant to make it sound like a question, but every time she was in front of her mother, she felt like *she* was the thirteen-year-old. "I'm moving back home." As she broke the news, she looked down at Andi, hoping at least *she* would be excited.

A huge smile broke over Andi's face. "Really? Really?" she shouted. She had been happy with just a surprise visit. But her sister moving back? For good? That was seriously awesome.

"Is that okay?" Bex asked. She ignored the glare coming from her mother.

"Of course it's okay!" Andi cried. "It's your home, too! Except your room is now an office slash home gym and we sold all your toe rings at a garage sale." As she said this, Andi shot her mother a look. She *had* told her that was a bad idea.

Before his wife could speak, Andi's father jumped in. "We have a pull-out couch," he said, squeezing Celia's shoulder. He could feel the tension and knew he would be in trouble later, but Bex was his daughter. He wasn't going to have her sleeping on the floor. "You can stay for as long as you want."

Bex smiled gratefully. "So, my plan is to get a job and find a place to live. I'm really ready to get my life together." She risked looking at her mother, thinking that perhaps the words *plan* and *job* might be enough to thaw the daggers of ice Celia had been shooting her way since the moment she walked into the kitchen. No such luck.

"Hmm," Celia said, cool as ever. "Why now?"

Bex looked at Andi and smiled. Reaching out, she tickled Andi's sides, making the younger girl laugh as she tried to squirm away. "Well, I don't want this one to grow up before I do."

"Too late for that," Celia said. Without another word, she turned and walked back up the stairs. A moment later, a door slammed.

Bex sighed. She walked to the staircase and peered up at the empty hallway. "Wow! Very dramatic exit, Mom," she shouted. "You still got it." She sighed. Then she looked back at her father and Andi, who were standing there silently. She shrugged. She hadn't been home even twenty minutes and already she wanted to run away. But she tamped that feeling down. She was staying. She hadn't been lying about her plan, even if her mom didn't like it.

A part of Bex knew she should have been prepared for that reaction. But a part of her had hoped that maybe, just maybe, this time things would be different.

She wanted a fresh start. For her and for her mom. Most important, she had come home because she wanted a fresh start with Andi. But she wasn't sure that could ever happen if her mom was going to keep this up. . . .

CHAPTER 3

Andi loved her room. She loved the big canopy bed and the soft purple paint on the walls. She loved the bookcases, lined with books and the odds and ends she had collected over the years, like her buffalo stuffed animal and the birdhouse she had made in second grade. But most of all, she loved that the room *wasn't* perfect. It was perfectly *im*perfect. Her mom had agreed to let her decorate the way she wanted to, so unlike the rest of the house, her room was a bit bohemian. A little like Bex, Andi thought as she sat on her bed, making a bracelet. When things got tense, or she just needed to get away, that was what Andi did: she made things.

Hearing a knock on her door, she looked up. Bex was standing in the doorway. "Hey, you busy?"

"No," Andi said, smiling, "just messing around."

Taking that as an invitation to come in, Bex walked over and jumped onto the bed with Andi.

"Oh!" she said, seeing the combination of red plastic and string in Andi's hand. "What's this?"

"It's a straw and a shoelace," Andi said. She had cut up a red straw into one-inch pieces and woven the shoelace back and forth through them. The result was a bracelet that looked a lot more punk rock than drinking instrument.

Holding it in her hand, Bex ran her fingers over the plastic and bent it back and forth, surprised by how well put together it was. "You just turned a straw and a shoelace into a bracelet?" she asked, looking up at Andi with admiration.

Andi smiled proudly. She never got tired of making things or of people liking them. Buffy and Cyrus teased her whenever she said it was easy. They pointed out that *they* couldn't just pick up an old shoebox and turn it into a fantastic jewelry box. They didn't see objects that way. But Andi did. She always had. She jumped off the bed and grabbed a few things off her desk. "Look at this," she said, joining Bex again. "Anything can be a bracelet. Comic books, soda tabs." As she spoke, she showed her sister some of the other bracelets she had made. The comic book bracelet was one of her favorites. She had cut the bright panels out in strips and used colorful duct tape to connect them all. The result was a wide bangle she could slip on and off her wrist. She held out one last bracelet. It was thin and wiry. "I *think* this is my old retainer," she said, then quickly added, "which, if Mom asks, I'm still wearing at night."

Bex laughed. "What do you do, just take stuff out of the trash?" she asked.

Andi nodded. "Hello! Carbon footprint? Future generations? And bonus: it drives Mom *crazy*." As she spoke, she turned to make sure her mother wasn't standing outside the door. It was one thing to say something like that when her mom couldn't hear, but she was pretty sure that was *not* the day to get caught.

Her sister laughed again and nodded. "Yeah, I'll bet." Holding the red straw bracelet up, Bex hesitated. Andi watched, wondering what would make her usually outgoing and fearless sister seem suddenly shy. Was it the mention of Mom? *Had* her mom shown up in the doorway behind her? Turning again, she let out a breath. No one was there. Still. *Phew.* Finally, Bex spoke. "Could I have this?"

Andi was surprised. That was not what she had expected to hear. She shook her head. "No, let me make you something special."

"This *is* special," Bex said, lifting the bracelet. "I love it." She placed it on her wrist. Next to her leather and silver bangles, it seemed super bright. But it looked perfect on her. Leaning on the arm with Andi's bracelet, Bex looked at the top of the bed. Dozens of scarves crisscrossed over one another, combining to form a riot of colors and a warm and cozy canopy. "Did you make this, too?" Bex asked, drawing her finger along one of the scarves.

"Yeah," Andi said. Now she was the one to act a bit shy as she added, "Out of the scarves you sent me." Every time Andi had gotten a scarf, it had been a way to connect with her sister. No matter how far away Bex was, or how different her life was, Andi could look up at her canopy and feel like they were together. Bex looked touched as Andi began to recall the various places the scarves had come from.

"Look," Andi said, brushing her fingers against the bright material that hung over them. "Mardi Gras, the Texas state fair, that music festival where people supposedly get naked . . ." Bex quickly looked away.

"Did *you*?" Andi asked, unable to help herself.

Bex flushed. "No, come on!" she protested. "You know me better than that!"

Andi frowned. "I really don't," she replied, saying out loud what she had been thinking just moments earlier.

Andi realized that while she had pieces of Bex's life and travels literally hanging over her, she really didn't know her big sister. Not that well, at least.

"That's true," Bex said, looking thoughtful. "You don't. But I can fix that." She jumped off the bed and ran out of the room.

Confused, Andi watched her go. Why, if her sister was trying to help Andi get to know her better, would she run away?

* ★ *

Bex dashed down the hall toward her bedroom. Or rather, the room that *used* to be her bedroom. Andi hadn't been kidding when she said that their parents had turned it into a home gym. A giant elliptical machine took up most of the space, and instead of books on the bookshelf, there were sets of weights, a yoga mat, and some strange-looking circle things that Bex thought *might* have something to do with Pilates.

Walking in, she saw her mother pedaling and pulling frantically on the elliptical. Not even saying hello, Bex beelined for her brown duffel bag. What she was looking for was right on top. She picked up the old wooden box and clutched it to her chest. She couldn't wait to show Andi what was inside. The box held so many memories—and secrets.

"No, no, no!"

Celia leapt off the elliptical, her shouts startling Bex. Pushing past Bex, she shut the door before her daughter could leave. Bex rolled her eyes. Leave it to her mother to be overly dramatic. She could paint the walls a tranquil blue and play spa music all she liked, but the woman was strung as tight as a tightrope.

"Andi never sees what's inside this box," Celia said, tapping the brown lid.

Bex furrowed her brow. "It's just pictures," she said, though she knew even as she said it that her mother would disagree—which she did, quickly.

"They're not *just* pictures." Celia gave her daughter a meaningful look. "It's secrets. Things she doesn't need to see . . . or know. . . ." Her voice trailed off, and for a moment the room was silent.

Bex looked down at the box in her hand. Her mom was right. The box *did* hold secrets. But what if it was time to share some of them? Didn't she have the right to show Andi? She felt her mother's hard gaze on her and looked up. Sighing, she nodded. "Okay, Mom," she agreed, holding up her hand. "I won't show her the box."

"Thank you," Celia said as she watched Bex walk over, put the box back in the bag, and then leave the room. Satisfied her daughter had made the right decision, Celia followed, then headed downstairs for some water.

She didn't see Bex turn and dash back into the room as soon as she was out of sight. Bex grabbed the box and headed back to Andi's room. Was it really that big of a deal that she had told a teensy, tiny, little white lie? It wasn't the first time, and it probably wouldn't be the last. What her mom didn't know wouldn't hurt her. And it wouldn't hurt Andi, either—she hoped.

Bex burst back into Andi's room, leapt onto the bed, and presented the box. "This is like my diary," she said, placing her long fingers on the lid. "You can't tell anyone anything you see in here. Okay?"

Andi nodded, her eyes wide. Bex had never, ever done anything like that before. Her visits had always been short. Andi had never had the chance to go deep with her sister, to really get to know her. Now she was sharing her "diary"? It was awesome.

Slowly, Bex pulled back the lid. Inside the box was a collection of odds and ends. A woven bracelet, ticket stubs, a sparkly frog sticker, and pictures. Lots and lots of pictures. Andi looked down at them, her mind racing. She wanted to know *everything*—and *everyone*. She reached in and pulled out a random Polaroid. "What about this guy?" she asked.

Bex looked at the photo and smiled. "Oh, that's Fletcher," she said, as though it were obvious. "He's a pirate, so I don't see him very often."

Andi's eyes narrowed as she tried to figure out if her sister was being serious. A pirate? Like Jack Sparrow? Or did she mean one of those horrible pirates who boarded oil tankers like in that movie with Tom Hanks? "A pirate?" she asked out loud.

Her sister gave her a teasing look. "I'm kidding," she said. "But he does have a boat. And a pet bird."

"So . . . pretty close?" Andi said, teasing her sister right back.

The two began to laugh, and Andi felt an unfamiliar rush of emotion. She wasn't sure what it was or what to call it, but it felt sort of like home. Or like finding out things about someone that made the picture of them much more focused. It was like, Andi finally decided, when a video stopped buffering and became clear. "Your life looks so amazing," she said.

"Uh, so does yours," Bex said, looking around the room.

Andi rolled her eyes. "Which part?" she asked. "The stuff I'm not allowed to do, the stuff I'm not allowed to eat, *or* the stuff I'm not allowed to wear?" As the words poured out of her mouth, Andi felt a twinge of guilt.

"Is it that bad?" Bex asked, concern in her eyes.

There was a semiserious moment as she waited for Andi's answer.

The younger girl smiled, pushing away the self-pity. She was never one to feel bad for long. Life was too short. That was something she had learned from her big sister. "It will be better with you here."

Bex nodded. "We'll hang out!" she said excitedly, putting the picture of Fletcher back in the box.

"It'll be fun," Andi agreed. "Maybe not Mardi Gras, music festival fun . . . but we can get pizza." She paused. "Well, sometimes. When Dad's in charge." Her mom considered pizza beneath her palate. She had even gone as far as to say it shouldn't be classified as food. Andi wholeheartedly disagreed. Pizza, in her opinion, was the food of gods.

"You know what? I'm already having fun," Bex said. "You made me a bracelet. I like your friends. I like your room." She jumped off the bed and landed in front of Andi's desk. Andi's laptop was open to her favorite social media page. The profile picture she had stopped on was of a cute boy. He was wearing a sports jersey and running across a grass field. "Ohhh . . . this guy looks like fun." Bex leaned down so she could get a better look. "'Jonah Beck,'" she read out loud.

Andi leapt off the bed. Grabbing the computer, she slammed it shut. "You didn't see that," she said, suddenly all nerves. "And I have homework." Andi held on to her computer as she sat back down on her bed.

"Okay, cool," Bex said, trying not to laugh at the girl's obvious reaction. She knew exactly why Andi had been looking at that picture and exactly why she was suddenly a mess. Somebody had a crush. But she wouldn't push it. She also knew Andi would tell her about that Jonah guy when she was ready. "Andi, calm down."

As Bex leaned over, Andi pushed herself back against the headboard, clutching the computer to her chest. She was pretty sure that her heart was beating so hard it was making the laptop bounce.

"Okay, okay, I'll go unpack," Bex said, raising her hands in surrender. At the door, she turned and added, "Enjoy your picture of Jonah Beck." Laughing, she left.

Behind her, Andi sighed. That had been too close for comfort. Bex was *not* supposed to have seen that. *No one* was supposed to have seen that. Jonah Beck was like her own version of Bex's diary box. He was a secret. Or at least her crush on him was supposed to be a secret. True, Buffy and Cyrus knew that she had been crushing on him since the first day she had seen him. But who wouldn't have a crush on Jonah, with his brown hair that fell in front of his gorgeous blue eyes—and the dimples?

She opened the computer and stared at the screen in front of her. Yup, Jonah Beck was dreamy. And for then, at least, he was still her secret.

CHAPTER 4

"You didn't have to get me a birthday present."

Andi was officially thirteen. The sun was shining. The sky was blue and the air was perfect—not too warm but warm enough for shorts and her favorite T-shirt, the white one with the dog face on the front.

So far the day was shaping up to be exactly what she wanted. She and her family had had breakfast—together—and then she had gotten her presents, and then, to her surprise, Bex had told her to get in the car. Now she found herself walking through the big park at the center of town, not sure what was going on but enjoying more time with her sister.

"Well, I'm not sure it's going to top what Mom got you . . ." Bex started. Then she stopped and laughed.

Her mother had gotten Andi *The Unabridged History of Math.* "Oh, wait, it *is* going to top that." She looked toward a small rise in the field. As if on cue, the present appeared at the top of the rise. "Here it comes . . ." she said, smiling.

As Andi turned to follow Bex's gaze, her mouth dropped open. Then it closed. Then it dropped open again. She felt like a fish out of water. She couldn't breathe. Because there, running toward them with a huge smile on his perfectly dimpled face and a Frisbee in his hands, was none other than Jonah Beck.

"Wh-wh-what did you do?" Andi stammered, dragging her eyes from Jonah to look up at Bex. Her heart was pounding, and her palms suddenly felt sweaty, and she was pretty sure she was going to throw up.

Bex, apparently oblivious to the torturous effect her "present" was having on Andi, grinned. "He's going to teach you how to play Frisbee. I got you a lesson. That's your present!"

Andi felt her head shaking back and forth, but it was as though she had no control over the motion. Nor did she have control over the string of noes that poured out of her mouth. Was her sister serious? This was the worst idea ever. In the history of ideas. The absolute worst.

"Just relax," Bex said, realizing that the stammering and headshaking were indications that Andi was having her own version of a meltdown. Andi got out another no. "Great. Just like that. Only the exact opposite." Before Bex could offer up any more advice, Jonah stopped in front of them.

Andi tried to act normal. But it was hard. Up close, Jonah Beck was even more perfect. He was smiling broadly, revealing straight white teeth, and his dimples were even more . . . dimply. Despite his sprint across the field, he was breathing evenly, and not a hair was out of place on his head, except for the adorable bangs that fell over his right eye.

"Hi," Bex said, ignoring the sounds of hyperventilating coming from Andi. "You Jonah?" The boy nodded. "Great, I'm Bex. And this is your student, Andi."

Jonah's smile grew broader. Pushing up the sleeves on his zip-up hoodie, he nodded. "Dude," he said, "I know you. You go to Jefferson, right?"

Andi opened her mouth and tried to answer. But to her horror, nothing came out.

Luckily, Bex was able to say yes for her, and Jonah didn't seem to notice the sudden onset of mutism. "Cool," he said. "Some people never forget a face. I never forget a foot."

Andi followed his gaze to her feet. She was wearing a pair of sneakers she had put her own touch on by covering them completely with different colors of duct tape. The result? A pair of one-of-a-kind kicks that stood out in any crowd. At the compliment, Andi's heart stopped, which, given the intense pounding it had only moments before been doing, felt both great and terrible. Before she could even say thank you, Jonah went on.

"So what do you say? Ready to hurl?" he asked, holding up his bright orange Frisbee.

Andi's eyes grew wide. Was it that obvious?

* * *

To Andi's surprise, she spent the next hour of her thirteenth birthday *not* hurling. Instead, she found herself playing Frisbee—or at least trying to play Frisbee. And to her even greater surprise, she wasn't totally terrible at it. In fact, as the afternoon wore on, she realized that she was enjoying herself. And that Jonah was even cooler than she could ever have imagined.

He showed her how to throw the disk forehand, then backhand. He showed her how to lunge without pulling every muscle in her body. And while at first she really was bad—like throw-the-Frisbee-in-the-pond bad—with Jonah's help she got better. Soon she was jumping and chucking the disk like she had been doing it for months, not minutes.

As she exchanged a high five with Jonah after a particularly awesome catch, he lowered the Frisbee. "You're joining the team," he said excitedly. His dimples were even deeper, and his bright blue eyes were twinkling. "Say yes. Right now. Say it. Say 'Yes, I'm joining the team.'"

Andi couldn't help smiling at his enthusiasm. But she was confused. "What team?"

"The Ultimate Frisbee team. *Durr.* I'm the captain," Jonah explained.

Andi nodded. Right. She had known that. There was just one teensy, tiny problem. "That's a sport. I don't play sports. I'm an indoor person." Anyone who knew her knew she was much more comfortable at her workbench than on a playing field. Although to be fair, up until that day Jonah hadn't known more about her than that she made kickin' kicks.

But Jonah was proving to be as stubborn as he was adorable. "What if you're really an outdoor person?" he said, pressing her. "Listen. You're good at this."

Andi couldn't help smiling even as she said, "I am?" It *was* pretty sweet how enthusiastic he was about the whole joining-the-Frisbee-team thing. Still . . . even if Jonah thought she was good, she wasn't sure she was good enough to be part of an actual team.

Jonah, however, was not going to take no for an answer. He told her practice was the next day. "You know you like this," he said, finishing his plea.

"I like you," Andi said. She gasped, her eyes growing wide. She looked around, hoping that a hole had suddenly opened in the field for her to drop into. She hadn't meant to say that *out loud*. And she really hadn't meant to say that out loud *to Jonah*. Quickly, she tried to cover her massive oops. "I like *it*. I like *Frisbee*. Just delete what I said before."

Luckily, she was saved from further humiliation by the sound of footsteps. A moment later a girl threw herself onto Jonah's arm. "Amber alert," the girl said in a sickly sweet voice, tugging at the sleeve of his hoodie. "Amber alert."

Andi's eyes narrowed. The girl's long blond hair shone in the sun, and her eyes were nearly—but not quite—as bright blue as Jonah's. Instantly, Andi felt as though she had shrunk and grown a third eye. The girl, whoever she was, was clearly older and, judging from the way she kept touching Jonah's arm, clearly into him.

"Um, this is Amber," Jonah said. He looked uncomfortable as he said it, and Andi felt a brief flare of hope.

"His *girlfriend*," Amber added, dumping a big bucket of water all over Andi's hope.

"Hi. Nice to meet you," Andi said, hoping that the disappointment she was feeling wasn't written all over her face. Racking her brain for something to say, she added, "You guys are a cute couple. You don't go to Jefferson, because I'd remember that."

Amber raised one perfectly shaped eyebrow and gave Andi a look that clearly said, *Oh, well aren't you just the sweetest*, in a totally fake tone. Out loud, she informed Andi that she went to Grant. As in the high school.

There was an awkward pause as the two girls eyed each other and Jonah stared at the grass as though it were the most fascinating thing he had ever seen. Then, before things could get any more uncomfortable, Andi said a quick good-bye. She had had a good time with Jonah. He wanted her to join his Frisbee team. If she was being honest with herself, that was a pretty good end to the morning. After all, she hadn't even known she was going to be hanging with him that day. Still, there was something so smug about the way Amber was looking at her that it made her feel like she couldn't leave without saying one last thing. Brushing past the older girl, Andi paused long enough to say what she had been thinking since the girl first walked up. "By the way, AMBER Alerts are for kidnapped children. So more terrifying as opposed to cute. Just something to think about."

Without another word, Andi walked on. She could hear Bex calling her name, but she ignored her sister. She might have put on a smile in front of Jonah and Amber, but she was mortified. How could her sister have done that to her? How could she have set her up to look like a fool?

Catching up to her, Bex reached out and grabbed Andi's arm, forcing her to stop. Andi whirled on her. "He has a girlfriend—who's in high school!" she said after informing Bex how embarrassed she was. "Did you see her?"

"What?" Bex said, sounding genuinely confused. "So she's a pretty girl! She's nothing. She's not you!"

Andi wanted to scream. How could her sister be so oblivious? "You're right!" she said, raising her voice. "She's up here!" She lifted her arms as high as they would go and stood on her tiptoes for emphasis. Then she pointed to the ground. "And I'm down—move your foot—there. Where you were just stepping on."

"Stop. You obviously can't see yourself," Bex said softly.

"And you can?" Andi asked, her tone biting. Bex took a step back, a wounded look on her face. Andi felt a pang of guilt. She knew the comment had stung, but she had wanted someone else to hurt the way she was hurting right then—even if it was her sister. Andi turned and started to walk away.

Bex followed, a look of determination replacing the wounded one. "You were raised to think you have to be perfect," she said to Andi's back. Her voice rose. "But you don't." She wanted Andi to know that it was good to have moments like that, even if Andi didn't think so. Those moments, Bex said, finally getting the younger girl to stop, were the ones she would remember. They would be the funny stories she would tell people one day.

"That's you," Andi said, looking up at Bex. "That's not me."

"Not yet," Bex agreed. "I'm trying to help you."

Andi was done listening. She had heard enough. She knew exactly what her sister was trying to do, and she was over it. The emotions from the day— from the nervousness to the excitement to the final embarrassment—welled up like water behind a dam. And then the dam burst. "I don't need your help. You don't know how I feel. I'm not like you. I'm not cool or adventurous. I'm not one of those people in your memory box. Those are the people you know. I'm just some girl you send scarves to." She whipped around and took off across the field, leaving Bex and her "help" behind.

CHAPTER 5

Andi lay in her bed, staring up at the canopy of scarves. She had spent the rest of the day in her room alternating between feeling bad for yelling at her sister and being mad at her sister for sticking her nose where it didn't belong. Then she had received a text from Jonah. He had sent a picture of himself with a Frisbee. On the Frisbee he had drawn a face, and the text said *We miss you*. It was cute and sweet and had made Andi feel better—for a minute. Then she had gone right back to feeling terrible. Only now she was feeling terrible for being terrible . . . to Bex.

The light in the hallway went on, sending a beam into Andi's eyes. A moment later she heard someone banging around. Curious, she turned on her bedside lamp and got out of her bed. Walking down the hall, she saw that the door to the home gym/Bex's old room was open a crack. The noise was coming from inside. Pushing the door open, Andi saw Bex stuffing clothes into her duffel.

"Bex?" Andi said.

Bex turned. "Oh, great. I woke you," she said. She barely looked at Andi. Instead, she kept packing. "This has been a banner day. Don't worry, I'm leaving first thing in the morning."

"No, Bex, don't go," Andi said, walking over. "I take back what I said. Every word of it."

Bex paused her packing. She looked down at Andi. "You don't have to."

"But can I?" Andi said. Even as she spoke, she realized she should have said this hours earlier. It was what she had been thinking ever since she'd heard from Jonah. Really, it was what she had been thinking since she'd stopped and actually thought about what her sister had been trying to say. She took a deep breath and went on, figuring late was better than never. "You

were right. These *are* the moments I'll remember."
She paused. "Jonah Beck *texted* me. I don't even know
how he has my number."

To Andi's surprise, Bex smiled. "Don't be mad, but
I gave it to him," she said. "He asked for it."

"He did? Jonah Beck asked for my number?" Andi
said, practically squealing but then stopping when she
remembered her parents were asleep down the hall.
She lowered her voice. "That's an amazing sentence. I
need to say it again. Jonah Beck asked for my number?"

Bex laughed. "I'm just glad you're happy," she said,
looking at the glow on Andi's face.

"So you'll stay?" Andi said hopefully.

The laughter died on Bex's lips, and she looked
back down at her half-packed duffel. All she wanted
to do was say yes, that she would stay and be a part of
Andi's life. But if that day had been any indication, she
would probably just mess things up. That was what she
did. That was what she had always done. "I've made
too many mistakes," she finally said.

"When?" Andi asked, determined to keep her sister
from leaving.

"Today. And yesterday. And the day before that,"

Bex answered. "And every single day of your life." She turned and looked at Andi's hopeful face. Tears welled up in her eyes. Her heart pounded. She wanted to tell Andi the truth. She wanted so badly to tell her.

"What are you talking about?" Andi said, confused by the look on Bex's face. "You're scaring me."

Bex took a deep breath. She had made a promise a long time ago to her parents. But that had been then. This was now. And now things were different. She couldn't keep pretending. Thirteen years had been long enough. "You should be scared. Do you think that you're not in here?" Bex asked, taking the wooden box out from the duffel. "You are." Slowly, she opened the lid and popped open a hidden compartment on the top. A picture fell out.

Taking the picture in her hands, Andi looked down at it. Then she looked up at her sister. "Is that you?" she asked, even though she knew the answer. The Bex in the picture looked so young, her hair shorter and her face rounder. She was lying in a hospital bed, holding a baby in her arms.

Bex nodded. And then, slowly, she reached out and pointed at the baby in the picture. "And that's you," she said softly. "Andi, I'm not your sister . . . I'm your mother."

Andi looked up as her mouth dropped open. "You're my *what*?" she asked, this time not bothering to keep her voice down. She wasn't even sure why she had asked. She had heard Bex loud and clear.

"I'm your mother," Bex repeated, wringing her hands nervously.

Andi began to shake her head. This couldn't be happening. This wasn't happening. This was the kind of thing that happened in terrible daytime television shows. This didn't happen to her. She had a mom already. She had a mom whom she needed to see— right then. *"Mom!"* she shouted. *"Mooooom!"*

"Please," Bex said. "She's going to be so mad."

But it was too late. Celia burst into the room. She took one look at the two girls and the open box on the bed, then turned and yelled for her husband. Then she turned back and screamed at her older—or rather, only—daughter. "You had no right!"

"It just slipped out," Bex said, not sounding very convincing.

Bursting into the room, Andi's father looked at the gathered women. "What's going on?" he asked.

"My brain feels like it's melting!" Andi shouted as her parents—or the two people she had *thought* were her parents—began to yell at Bex. Over the pounding of her heart and the throbbing in her melting brain, she heard first her mother, then her father tell Bex she had had no right to say anything. Finally, Andi couldn't take it anymore. "You don't get to be upset," she erupted, pointing at Celia. Then she pointed at Ham. "You don't get to be upset." Finally, she looked at Bex. "And you don't get to be upset. The *only* person who gets to be upset here is me. Because you all have been lying to me. For my *whole life*." She looked one by one at the three people whom, up until a few minutes earlier, she had trusted completely. The people who had said they loved her and would never, ever hurt her. She narrowed her eyes. Well, the joke was on her. Because they had just hurt her—a lot.

She turned and raced out of the room. She had to get as far away from her "family" as she could.

✳ ✳ ✳

Andi ran to the one place that had always brought her comfort: Andi Shack. It was a small house in the backyard, and she had made it her own over the years, filling the small space with her craft supplies and finished projects. The result was a cozy space that was completely and totally hers. Paper lanterns hung from the ceiling. Uninflated balloons in a variety of colors covered the wood paneling, and a thick branch strung with colored duct tape hung over the window as a makeshift window treatment. A big shaggy rug lay on the floor, and dozens and dozens of jars of every shape and size were filled to the brim with things like pipe cleaners and paintbrushes. All things that had always made her happy.

But now, as she lay inside on her futon, struggling to stop her brain from melting, she couldn't even find comfort in the comfortable. Her parents were her grandparents? Her sister was her mother? Everything she had ever known was one giant lie. Even her shack was a lie. It had probably been a gift from her parents/grandparents to try to make up for the fact that every time they opened their mouths, they were lying. Her brain melted some more.

Hearing a sound outside the small half door, she raised her head off the pink pillow and saw Bex hovering uncertainly on the threshold.

"Please don't touch anything," Andi said, slowly sitting up. The movement made her head hurt more, and she knew the frown on her face was deep.

Bending down, Bex peered at the small homemade lamp by Andi's futon. "Are those my CDs?" she asked. The silver circles were glued together to form an octagon that housed a single bulb. Andi shrugged and apologized. Bex nodded. So that was how it was going to be? She couldn't blame Andi. She honestly couldn't begin to imagine what the girl was thinking or feeling. But she had just admitted she was Andi's mom. And as her mom, she had to try to make things better. "Andi, I'm so, so sorry."

"Just stop," Andi said, not letting her continue. "It's too weird. When I look at you, I see my cool sister, out in the world, having adventures on her motorcycle." She shook her head. "But that's not who you are. You're my mother—who abandoned me." As she spoke, the tears she had been fighting welled in her eyes. She tried to hold them back, not willing to let her sister/mother see how much she was hurting.

Bex, however, did not seem to mind letting Andi know *she* was hurting. Her own eyes filled with tears as she began to shake her head. "That's not what happened," she said. "Do you want to know what happened?"

"No." The word sounded loud in the small space. "Not right now," Andi clarified. Because she *did* want to know. She wanted badly to know.

"Whenever you're ready," Bex said, honoring Andi's wishes. "I'll tell you everything. Whatever you want to know."

"I just want to think about my text from Jonah right now," Andi said, dropping her head into her hands. Even through the misery of the situation, saying the words *text* and *Jonah* in the same sentence made her feel a little bit better.

Looking at Andi's lowered head, Bex nodded slowly. "I think that's a great idea," she said. Then she stood up and turned to go. She walked the few steps toward the door, her shoulders stooped and her face fallen. Knowing how much pain Andi was in was more terrible than anything she could have imagined. Pausing at the door, she turned back. "You probably hate me. You probably should hate me," she said softly. "But I'll always love you. And I always have. And you have that whether you want it or not." Pushing the door open, she walked outside, letting the tears finally fall.

Behind her, Andi lowered her head to the pillow— and let her own tears fall.

CHAPTER 6

Andi had been convinced the world was over, but the sun still rose the next morning, and the alarm still went off bright and early, reminding her that while she now had a mother she had thought was a sister, she still had school. That meant she would have to see her best friends, and she had no idea what she was going to say. Should she tell them? Should she keep it a secret? She really wasn't sure she was ready to tell them yet, but if she kept it a secret, was she any better than her own family? Sighing, she decided to just get on the bus and see what happened.

Arriving in front of Jefferson Middle School, she instantly spotted Buffy and Cyrus standing by the bike racks. Cyrus was wearing her helmet and holding on to the seat of the bright yellow scooter. As she walked up, she heard him attempting to throw out some biker lingo. Laughing, she jumped between her friends. "You brought the bike! Thanks!" she cried as Cyrus tried to remove the helmet and ended up nearly choking himself.

"You ready to take off the training wheels?" Buffy asked.

Andi shrugged. "I'm not even sure I'm keeping it."

Buffy gave her friend a look. "Did something happen on your birthday?" she asked. "I tried calling you all day."

"Yeah, me too," Cyrus said. "No answer."

Andi knew her friends' prying was out of genuine concern. But now that she was at school, she knew she had to wait to tell them. "Yeah," she finally said. "Something happened. Something really, really big."

Buffy's eyes grew wide. "Are you going to tell us?" she asked, curiosity written all over her face.

Looking at the students hanging around and walking to class, Andi shook her head. "I can't just blurt it out right here."

"Why not?" Buffy asked.

Cyrus, who had been uncharacteristically quiet, finally jumped in. "Buffy!" he said. "Are you not listening? Something big happened. She's a totally different person." Buffy rolled her eyes at his over-dramatic synopsis of the conversation she had just been a part of. Ignoring his friend, Cyrus gave Andi a sympathetic look. "We know what you're trying to tell us. You don't need to spell it out."

For one brief moment, Andi wondered if somehow Cyrus *did* know. But then she shook her head. There was no way. "Trust me. You don't," she said. Hearing the bell, she turned and began to walk toward the school entrance. "I gotta go. It's my first period."

"Exactly!" Cyrus said, mistaking Andi's school schedule for what he had been convinced was her big news.

Throwing him a look, Andi shook her head. She loved her friend, but sometimes he came up with the craziest stories. Although none of his stories could come close to what she was going to tell him when she finally shared her news.

✵ ✱ ✽

The rest of the school day dragged by. Between trying to keep her secret and the three pop quizzes her teachers sprang on them, Andi was convinced she was never going to make it through the afternoon. But finally, the bell rang.

She grabbed her backpack and books, then sprinted out the front doors and toward the playing field. There was one other thing she hadn't told her friends yet: she was going to play on the Ultimate Frisbee team . . . with Jonah Beck.

The rest of the team was already gathered when Andi arrived, but Jonah spotted her instantly. His face broke into a huge smile, and he raced over. "You came!" he said.

"I'm still not sure about this," Andi said, glancing at the field, where players were running drills. Cones were set up all over the place, and everyone seemed to know exactly what they were doing. She was going to make a fool of herself if she went through with joining. But then she looked back at Jonah. To her surprise, he was holding up a T-shirt with a number thirteen on the back, and over the number was written *ANDIMAN*.

"How'd you come up with that?" she asked, pointing to the name.

Jonah shrugged. "Isn't that what everyone calls you?" he asked.

While his question was innocent, it hit Andi straight in the gut. Because it wasn't true. Not everyone called her that. "Just one person," she said. *Just my sister . . . or my mother . . .* she added silently.

Unaware of what Andi was thinking or feeling, Jonah gave her another huge smile. "Well, now it's two," he said. "Get out there, Andiman. This disk isn't going to catch itself."

Laughing, Andi ran out onto the field. Maybe she wasn't exactly a sports girl, but after her birthday, she wasn't really sure who she was anymore. And as the practice sped by and she found herself enjoying playing, she realized there was something kind of freeing in that. So when the practice ended, she didn't go right home like she had promised her mother— or rather, her grandmother. Instead, she took the training wheels off the scooter and hit the road. It was time she started being true to herself—whoever that was.

"Well, that's new," Celia said as Andi turned into the driveway a short while later.

Andi jumped off the scooter, took off her helmet, and shook her bangs out of her face. Before her birthday, she had been terrified of Celia's reaction. But that had been the old Andi. "I got an electric scooter. Do you like it?" the new Andi asked, smiling and walking over to where Celia was watering her plants.

"No, I don't," Celia answered.

Andi kept smiling. "It's super safe. It only goes like twelve miles an hour."

"Still no," Celia said.

At that point in the conversation, the old Andi would have backed down. But if she had learned anything from the day before, it was that honesty was better than lies. So instead, she shrugged. "Well, I wish you didn't feel that way," she said sincerely. "But I'm keeping it."

A look of concern crossed Celia's face as Andi brushed past her and continued up the walk to the front door. Celia had known there would be fallout from what Bex had revealed. But a suddenly rebellious Andi? That was *not* good. "Andi," Celia called, causing her to stop and look back. "I know you feel your world has been turned upside down. But I'm still in your life. Everything works just like it always has. Nothing has changed."

Andi raised an eyebrow. "Sure, nothing's changed," she said, then added, "Grandma." Zinger thrown, she turned and walked up the stairs, then disappeared through the front door.

Celia watched her go. "'Grandma'?" she repeated under her breath. Oh, Bex was going to get it. She had a whole lot more to answer for than telling Andi the truth. She had to answer for turning Celia into a grandmother overnight!

❀ ❀ ❀

Up in her room, Andi sat on her bed, trying to focus on the homework in front of her. Unfortunately, the numbers on the page were blurring together and all she could think about was Jonah. And her mom/sister/grandmother drama. And Jonah again. It was hard not to think about him—or his dimples.

Hearing a knock on the door, she looked up. Bex was hovering in the hallway, holding her brown keepsake box. Andi hadn't seen her since their conversation the night before, and she wasn't sure what Bex was going to say now.

"Remember when you said you wanted to make me something special?" Bex asked, surprising Andi. "Is that offer still good?"

"Sure," Andi said, tapping her pencil against her notebook. "But I'm kind of busy." The truth was she would have loved any excuse not to do her homework, but she didn't want to just say yes. She felt like she should make Bex wait.

Taking the "sure" as an invitation, Bex walked into the room. She sat down next to Andi on the bed, putting the brown box between them. She had traded her thicker choker for one made of a thin brown rope with a single bead dangling from it. Andi focused on the bead, happy to avoid making eye contact. "I wanted to be able to wear this again," Bex said, taking out a hospital bracelet.

Gingerly, Andi took it and looked down at the small white piece of plastic. *Mack, Rebecca* was written across it. Bex reached back into the box, pulled out a second bracelet, and handed that one to Andi, as well. Her name and date of birth were printed across that one, and the ID number was the same as the one that had been Bex's.

"Can I see that picture again? Of us?" Andi asked, the hardness around her heart softening. Seeing her baby bracelet and knowing that Bex had kept it all that time made it all seem more real, more genuine. She might have accused Bex of abandoning her, but Bex had clearly never forgotten her. Feeling Bex's eyes on her, Andi looked up and gave her a tentative smile. Then she looked back at the box. Her eyes narrowed. "Wait a second. You have pictures of all of your boyfriends in here?"

"Pretty much," Bex said.

"I wonder which one is my dad . . ." Andi said, beginning to search through the pictures.

Bex didn't give her a chance to search for long. Grabbing the box, she slammed the lid shut and began to back away from the bed. "Hey, who wants pizza?" she asked, trying—and failing—to distract Andi.

"You said you would tell me everything when I'm ready," Andi pointed out.

"I know I did. It's just that you're not . . ." Bex stopped herself. She wasn't going to lie to Andi anymore. Not even about something like this. "*I'm* not ready," she finished.

Andi nodded. "Just let me know when you are," she said. Smiling, Bex turned and left the room, taking the box with her. Andi waited until Bex was out of sight before lifting the baby bracelet up. Turning it over in her hands, she marveled at how small it was. So much had happened in the thirteen years since it had been wrapped around her wrist.

Slowly, a smile crept over her face. She still had a lot of questions. And she still wanted answers. But she was beginning to think that maybe this wasn't a bad thing after all. Maybe this was the beginning of a wonderful new adventure. Maybe this was one of those moments Bex had described—a moment she would tell people all about . . . someday.

CHAPTER 1

Andi Mack had spent the first thirteen years of her existence believing her life was pretty normal. Overprotective but loving mom? Check. Kind and laid-back dad? Check. Cool older sister? Check. She lived in a nice house in a beautiful town and had two best friends who were awesome, caring, and fun. She went to a good school and got decent grades, had a kicking shack in her backyard where she got to create all sorts of crazy crafts, and was, for the most part, usually happy. She even had a crush on the cutest boy at Jefferson Middle School. Also completely normal.

And then she discovered that her family had been lying to her—her entire life. Turns out the overprotective but loving mom and kind dad she had always thought of as her parents were actually her *grand-parents*. And her sister? Well, it turned out her sister, Bex, was actually her *mother*. And the biggest kicker? She found out all of this on her thirteenth birthday after an epic fight with Bex and a totally amazing day with her crush, Jonah Beck.

Over the next few weeks, she had time to come to grips with her new reality—sort of—and was even beginning to feel kind of okay about it all. Kind of. There were still some things to work out, like what to call the person she'd thought was her mother. Was she Celia now? Or Grammy? Or something else entirely? And what was she supposed to tell people when everyone finally found out? Her family lived in a small town. It was only a matter of time before someone put it all together. But there was one big thing that had been hanging over her since she had found out the truth, and it bothered Andi more than she let on. While she now knew who her mother was, she still had no idea who her dad was—not yet, anyway. Every time she tried to bring it up, Bex would change the subject, or order pizza. Granted, Andi loved a good pizza, but even she was growing tired of the cheesy, bready goodness. She just wanted the truth. Wasn't that the least her sister—*mother*—could do after lying to her for thirteen years?

Wandering into the living room, which Bex was currently using as her bedroom, Andi found her folding clothes. Having just been told by her grandmother—which still felt funny to say—that she couldn't have sweets before dinner, her eyes landed on a box of sugary toaster pastries that was randomly lying on the pull-out. Reaching out to grab one, she was surprised when Bex snatched the box away. Andi's eyes narrowed. Since when had Bex been on the whole "don't eat this" thing, too?

In one smooth move, Andi pulled the box out of Bex's grasp. Holding the open end over her other hand, she shook it. To her surprise, a photograph, not a Toaster Tart, fell onto her palm. Her eyes grew wide as she looked down at the picture of a guy. "Is this my father?" she asked, looking up at Bex.

"No," Bex said. The short answer was unusual for Bex, and it only made Andi more suspicious.

Narrowing her eyes, she held out the picture. "Then who is it?"

"Nobody," Bex answered.

Andi shook her head. Usually, her long dark bangs would have fallen in her face, but that morning she had pulled them back with a new barrette she had made. She thought the silver geometric shape looked nice with her blue bunny sweater. It also helped not to have to constantly, in moments like this, be pushing the hair out of her eyes. "You don't put *nobody* in a Toaster Tart box," she said. "You told me that you took my dad's picture out, and then I find this picture. Nobody . . . is *somebody*." Ignoring the look on Bex's face, which screamed *drop it*, Andi pressed on. "Who. Is. It?" she asked again.

Bex just shook her head. Tugging at the bottom of her plaid button-down, she stood quietly for a moment. Then, before Andi could stop her, she reached out and grabbed the photograph. Walking over to the wastebasket, she ripped the picture into shreds, dropping the small pieces into the bin as she went. "See? Nobody," she said. Pulling her phone out of the back pocket of her jeans, she swiped open the screen. "Who wants pizza?"

Andi watched as Bex began to dial. Her mouth pulled back in a crooked, knowing smile. Bex could rip up pictures and say it was "nobody" all she wanted, pretending it was all nothing. But the pizza and the overdramatic actions? They screamed that it was the exact opposite. This was very much *something*. "I know for a fact that he *is* somebody," she said, stopping Bex mid-dial, "because you bring up pizza every time you don't want to answer my questions. But it's not going to work this time." Then her stomach rumbled. Figuring out her new life was not only exhausting, but it made her hungry, too. Sighing, she shrugged. "Except now I'm hungry."

"Half plain, half pepperoni?" Bex asked, seeing her chance and taking it.

"Extra cheese," Andi clarified. Then, lifting her chin, she narrowed her eyes. Bex might have won this round, but Andi wasn't going to let her off the hook for good. She was going to get answers. She was going to find out who her father was one way or another. Even if it meant eating pizza every day for the next year.

✴ ✴ ✴

Sitting at the counter of The Spoon, Shadyside's best—and only—diner, Buffy played absently with her food. She wasn't really that hungry, but she had told Cyrus she would meet him there, and as usual, he was running late. Since she had never been good at doing nothing, she had gone ahead and ordered food. At least eating gave her something to do.

Hearing a commotion, she turned and saw Cyrus weaving his way around the tables of the crowded diner. Reaching the counter, he stopped, playing up his dramatic entrance to the fullest. "Guess what just happened?" he asked.

Buffy eyed her friend. He was breathing heavily, and his face was flushed. Actually, it seemed like only *one* side of his face was red. She cocked her head and waited for the explanation she was sure to get.

"I ran into a glass door!" Cyrus said, sounding oddly pleased by the news.

"Again?" Buffy asked.

Cyrus nodded. "A different one!" he said, as though that made the fact that he had a habit of running into doors completely reasonable and not at all concerning. "Much more painful!" he added.

"Then why are you so happy?" Buffy asked. He was smiling broadly and didn't seem to be in any kind of pain.

As Cyrus started to answer, Andi walked in and joined them, seating herself at the counter. Looking back and forth between her two best friends, she tried to figure out what was going on. Cyrus was saying something about adrenaline, and Buffy was giving him one of her signature eye rolls. Then Cyrus put his hand to his face and began to moan. Throwing himself across the counter, he let his moans grow louder. Looking over at Buffy, Andi raised an eyebrow.

"He ran into a glass door," Buffy explained.

"Oh," Andi said, nodding. That sounded about right. Swiveling on her stool, Andi listened to her friend's moans and tried not to laugh. Cyrus was an amazing best friend. He was kind and sweet and always willing to listen to her talk about boys and help with her crafts. But he *could* be a bit over the top. Like now, for example. As she swiveled around, Andi realized she and Buffy weren't the only ones paying attention to Cyrus's whining. Everyone in the restaurant—which was full of students at this hour—was looking at them.

"People are staring at you," Andi said under her breath.

"Actually, they're staring at *you*," Buffy corrected.

Andi's eyes grew wide as she realized her friend was right. Frantically, she began to check herself all over. The bottoms of her feet. Her shoulders. The straps on her suspenders. The front of her black-and-red striped top. Had she spilled something? Was there something in her hair? "Is it toilet paper? Wardrobe malfunction?" she asked, looking to her friends for help. Then she lifted her chin so Buffy could check her nose for cliffhangers.

"You're clean," Buffy said.

While Andi had been freaking out, Cyrus had grown oddly quiet. His moans had stopped, and his cheeks—both of them this time—reddened. Gulping, he looked at his friends. "Um . . ." he began nervously. "I don't know if this is related, but I *might* have possibly mentioned to my mom about Bex being your mom."

"Cyrus!" Andi and Buffy said at the same time. "It was a secret!" Buffy admonished.

Andi's heart thudded in her chest. She had known this moment would come sooner or later. It was inevitable. But she had sort of hoped it would come on her own terms. Not because her best friend went and spilled the secret—*her* secret—to his mom. Andi felt the weight of everyone's eyes on her back, and she wanted to melt through the stool and down into the floor of The Spoon.

"I thought I was helping you," Cyrus said, the explanation sounding weak.

"Why would you think that?" Andi asked, agitated. She had been nervous about sharing the secret with Buffy and Cyrus in the first place. But then she had realized that if she didn't tell them, she was no better than her own family. So she had gathered the courage and given them the news. They had both been wonderful about it—although rightly curious and a bit intrigued—and promised to help her keep it quiet until she was ready. She wasn't quite sure how Cyrus telling his mother accomplished that.

Cyrus quickly tried to justify his actions. "Look, it was hard for you just to tell us. You shouldn't have to go through that over and over." Andi frowned at him. He *did* make a good point. But still . . .

"But your mom is the biggest gossip," Buffy pointed out, saying out loud what Andi had been thinking. "She probably told everyone."

Cyrus nodded, suddenly looking pleased. "She *definitely* told everyone," he agreed. "Sent out an email blast, and *boom*, it's done. The hard part is over."

Andi sighed. She wished she could believe Cyrus about the hard part being over. But if she knew anything about being a middle schooler, it was that kids were brutal. They latched on to gossip like a burr. "I just replaced the girl who tried to run herself up the flagpole as the school freak."

"I'm sorry," Cyrus said softly, looking down at the counter. He truly had been trying to help. Trying to lighten the mood—which had grown decidedly darker in the past few moments—he lifted a hand to his face. "Boy, is my face half-red," he joked. "Get it? 'Cause I ran into the . . ." His voice trailed off as he was met with blank stares from Buffy and Andi. "Never mind."

And then, just when Andi thought things couldn't get any more awkward or embarrassing, Jonah Beck walked into The Spoon. She bit back a groan. Now would have been a really good time for a hole in the floor to appear.

"What am I supposed to do? Where am I supposed to go?" Andi knew she sounded crazy, but at that moment, she didn't particularly care. Jonah Beck, the cutest boy in Jefferson Middle School, whom she had a serious crush on and who'd only recently learned her name, was walking toward her. All eyes were on him as he weaved through the tables and stopped at the counter. He gave Andi a smile. Andi tried not to swoon as his dimples flashed. His bright blue eyes were staring at her intensely. She shifted on her stool.

"Hi, Jonah," she said, trying to sound like she wasn't mentally freaking out and instead sounding disappointed to see him.

"Hey," he said, nodding in greeting. Since Andi had joined the Ultimate Frisbee team—at Jonah's request—they had become friends, sort of. But they didn't really hang out or talk much off the playing field.

Andi cocked her head, waiting to hear why he had come over. *Please don't ask about my mom. Please don't ask about my mom,* she chanted silently.

"So. Your mom thing—"

Andi's stomach dropped, and so did her expression. "You heard," she said, shooting Cyrus a look. He was so going to pay for this later.

"Yeah," Jonah replied. Then a huge smile broke out on his face. "That's *soooo* awesome!"

Andi, who had been crafting an elaborate story about Cyrus's delusional mother who liked to make up things, felt her mouth drop open. She shook her head to be sure she wasn't hearing things. "It is?" she said, confused.

Jonah's smile grew even broader. "I'm so boring compared to you," he said.

Looking at him, Andi had to admit he *did* look impressed. Which just made this whole thing even crazier. Because why would Jonah Beck, who was hands down the least boring person she knew, think he was boring compared to *her*? It made zero sense. Maybe she had entered some alternate universe, like on one of those shows Ham liked to watch from time to time. Where things *seemed* completely normal but were actually totally out of whack.

"Can I take a selfie with you?" Jonah asked.

Yup, she thought as Jonah leaned over and put his arm around her, holding up his camera. *I'm definitely in some alternate universe.* But if this universe included Jonah Beck wanting a picture of the two of them, she was totally fine with it. Even if it meant everyone now knew her biggest secret.

CHAPTER 2

When Bex had come back to Shadyside for good, she had promised her parents she was going to get a job. She had told them she was going to be responsible. Grow up. But it turned out that getting a job and being a grown-up weren't exactly fun, and they also weren't easy. The only job she had been able to get was at a store on Main Street called The Fringe. It was full of clothes that Bex would have probably worn when she was Andi's age, and carried other random party favors, accessories, posters, and an oddly large assortment of hair dye. That was what Bex now found herself sorting by color at the request of her boss, Brittany—who happened to also be someone Bex used to babysit.

Hearing the jingle of the bell on the front door,

both Bex and Brittany looked up. "Customer," Brittany said to Bex. "Handle."

Bex bit her tongue. She had only been working at The Fringe for a few days, but she was already finding it a bit, well, *annoying*, to be given orders by someone a decade younger than she was. She had smiled through the "orientation" and rolled her eyes when Brittany explained the computer to her like she was senile, but she wasn't sure how much longer she was going to be able to take it.

Sighing, Bex nodded and headed to the door. To her surprise, she saw it was Andi. "Hey," Bex said happily. "What brings you here?"

Andi glanced around as though she were worried people might be hiding behind The Fringe's thick pink curtains to spy on her. Satisfied no one was listening—or watching—Andi leaned in close. "Jonah Beck knows," she said.

"Knows what?" Bex asked, confused.

Andi waggled her eyebrows. "About . . . you *know*," she said, putting emphasis on the "know," which did nothing to erase the look of confusion on Bex's face. "The *thing*. Us."

Bex had been dreading this moment since she had opened her big mouth and spilled the beans. She had been ready for her parents' anger. She had even anticipated that Andi would be upset. But she'd had zero idea how Andi would feel when other people began to find out. She looked closely, trying to read the younger girl's face.

"He said it was . . . *awesome!*" Andi let out a little squeal.

Bex let out the breath she hadn't realized she'd been holding. "Thank you, Jonah Beck!" She knew that in Andi's world, an endorsement from Jonah was as good as it got. "So . . . you're not mad at me anymore?" she asked hopefully.

"I'm not mad at you," Andi answered, ". . . right now." She wasn't willing to completely forgive Bex for the lying and the secrets and the pretending-she-was-her-sister-when-she-was-really-her-mother thing *quite* yet.

"I'll take it," Bex said. Then she paused as what Andi was saying finally sank in. "I can't believe you told him."

Andi shook her head. "I didn't," she said. "Cyrus

told his mom, so now it's out. Everyone knows."

"Everyone?" Bex repeated slowly. "As in *everyone*?" Her face went a few shades paler and her voice was shaky. Concern—and a solid amount of fear—filled her eyes. Pulling out her phone, she hit a number and then held it up to her ear. As Andi continued to tell her about all the different people who had come up to her during the day, telling her she was strong or offering the number of their family shrink, Bex listened to the phone ring on and on. Finally, it clicked, and she had a moment of hope, but then she groaned. "It's going straight to voicemail," she said, growing more and more worried. If her mother—Celia—knew that the secret was out . . . Bex shuddered. The thought was enough to send shivers of terror up and down her spine.

"Who are you calling?" Andi asked when she realized Bex was barely listening to her.

"Mom," Bex answered. "We've got to get home." Getting a surprisingly quick okay from her boss to leave work early, she grabbed Andi's hand.

Before Andi could ask any more questions or even protest, she found herself being dragged out of the store. She wasn't quite sure what was going on, but she was very sure that she had never seen Bex look quite so freaked out before.

❋ ❋ ❋

Unfortunately, despite her best efforts to get home before Celia found out the whole town knew she was not a mother of two daughters but rather a mother of one and a *grandmother* of another, Bex failed. It turned out Cyrus's mother's gossip reached far and fast, and it had taken only minutes for the Macks' neighbor—and an all-around busybody—to confront Celia. The neighbor had gotten hosed down, and Celia had ended up in need of a break from reality.

Walking in the front door, Bex found her parents on their way out, suitcases in hand. "Hey, guys," Bex said cautiously. "Everything okay, Mom?"

"What's with the luggage?" Andi added, nodding at the blue and black bags they parked at their feet.

"Your father seems to think I'm a menace to society," Celia said, answering both girls' questions. Her voice was oddly flat. And for someone whose husband had called her a menace, she seemed eerily calm.

Bex and Andi exchanged looks. "What happened?" Andi finally said. Even as she asked, though, she had a growing suspicion that whatever happened had something to do with Cyrus, his mom, and Shadyside's secret of the century getting out.

"Your mother engaged with a neighbor," Ham said, confirming Andi's suspicions.

Celia shook her head. "I was attacked," she clarified. "And the garden hose only reaches so far."

Andi cocked her head. She had never seen Celia like this. It was kind of . . . scary. Her eyes were cold, and her mouth was pinched so tight Andi was pretty sure she could see wrinkles forming. She leaned back a bit, as though it were only a matter of time before Celia exploded. Maybe going away for a while was a good idea.

Ignoring the looks both Andi and Bex were giving her, Celia rummaged around in her purse, making sure she had everything she needed. Then she looked up at Bex. "I'm trusting you," she said.

Bex smiled, surprised. Her mother had never left her home alone with Andi. "Thank you."

"I don't want to," Celia responded flatly. "Your father is forcing me." Without another word, she pulled up the handle on her suitcase and followed her husband toward the garage.

Silence descended over the kitchen. Sitting down on the stool next to Andi, Bex clasped her hands in front of her. She was still shocked her parents had left her in charge. And Andi was equally shocked that they had left Bex in charge—of her. Only a few days ago, Celia had been furious with Bex for letting Andi watch a scary movie. And now she was leaving them home alone? Whatever the neighbor had said must have been really, *really* bad.

"Well, kid," Bex finally said when the shock wore off, "it's just you and me. We can do whatever we want." Spreading her hands wide, she turned and smiled at Andi. "Got any ideas?"

Andi stared at the air in front of her, visions of freedom dancing in her head. Did she have any ideas? Ha! She had *soooo* many ideas! Where to begin? Did she want to stay up late? Did she want to have candy for breakfast? Or wear pajamas all day? Maybe not do her homework? She couldn't decide. The options were endless. "Let's have dinner in the living room," she finally said. "*While* we watch TV." That was a definite no-no when Celia was home. "And each have two desserts!" She looked over at Bex, pleased with her rebellious suggestions.

Bex frowned. "Okay, sure," she said, agreeing. "We can do that. But . . . think bigger," she suggested. Had Andi's life really been so controlled that dinner in front of the television was her idea of a great time?

"Scratch the dinner!" Andi said. "We'll just have dessert!"

Sighing, Bex put her hands down on the counter in front of her. It looked like she was going to have to spell things out for Andi. "Do you realize what just happened?" she said.

Andi shrugged and nodded. She *thought* she had realized. But from the look on Bex's face, she was beginning to think she had missed something.

"Mom and Dad are gone. *I'm* in charge," Bex said. Andi was still looking at her blankly. "Andi! Don't you get it? We can have a party!"

Andi tilted her head to the side. A party? She wasn't so sure that was the best idea. If Celia had been mad about a scary movie, a party would probably make her furious. There was no telling what she would do to Bex—and Andi—if she found out. And honestly, Andi wasn't sure she was willing to find out, even if a party *did* sound like fun. . . .

CHAPTER 3

While Andi was still pretty sure a party was a terrible idea, Bex, apparently, was not. In fact, she seemed pumped to party. Dragging Andi back to The Fringe, she began stocking up on all sorts of party favors and must-haves. Or, at least, that was what she called the boas and light-up accessories she was throwing into her basket.

"I really don't think this is a good idea," Andi said for the hundredth time as Bex grabbed a blond wig and a black-and-red cowboy hat.

"Look," Bex said. "You're getting older. There are some basic life skills you need to learn." She paused, weighing her options between blue and orange hats.

Shrugging, she added both to the basket. "One of them is giving a party."

Following Bex as she continued her shopping spree, Andi asked her, "Will I get a merit badge?"

Bex heard the sarcasm in Andi's voice but ignored it. "Yes," she said, "as a matter of fact, you will." She stopped in front of a set of shelves. Turning, she gave Andi a serious look. "You are fulfilling your responsibility to kids whose parents are not going out of town."

Before Andi could point out that she actually had *zero* obligation to those kids, Bex spotted something intriguing across the room. Letting out an excited "Ooh! Look!" she took off. Following her gaze, Andi saw the collection of masks and bunny-ear headbands. For the first time since Bex had suggested this harebrained idea, she was beginning to think this *could* be fun. After all, who didn't love an excuse to wear bunny ears?

"Was *this* your emergency?"

Brittany's high-pitched voice snapped Andi and Bex out of their accessory-fueled fun. Turning, they saw the girl standing with her arms crossed and her eyes narrowed. Bex gulped and shifted on her feet nervously. Andi's head swung back and forth as she looked between them, wondering what would happen.

"You *had* to have a party?" Brittany went on, nodding toward the baskets overflowing with party favors.

"Kind of?" Bex answered. She was worried. She really couldn't afford to lose a job she had *just* gotten. "I can explain—" she started to say.

"Don't bother," Brittany said, interrupting her abruptly.

Bex bit back a groan. She was going to get fired. In front of Andi. Talk about mortifying. And if Mom and Dad found out? She could just imagine the field day they would have with her most recent failure.

But to her surprise, Brittany kept going. "The whole mom thing?" she said, her frown fading, replaced by a look of curiosity. "Crazy! I just heard." She leaned closer. "Was it that guy who used to come over when you were babysitting?"

Andi's head snapped up. Had she just heard correctly? Bex used to babysit Brittany? That was odd. And probably a little bit awkward. But more important, there had been a guy? Who had hung out with Bex a lot? Maybe babysitting guy and Toaster Tart guy were the *same* guy!

From the frantic denials Bex was throwing out, Andi suspected she might be right. But before she could grill Bex, Brittany pointed at Andi. "Is this her?" she asked, holding out her hand. Bex nodded. "Hi, I'm Brittany."

Reluctantly, Andi took the girl's hand and shook it.

"Those glasses over there," Brittany said, turning her attention from the mother/daughter news to the more pressing party planning, "are great. They just came in."

As Andi watched, Bex, rejuvenated by Brittany's approval, resumed her shopping. She threw everything from ninja suits to black-light paint into her basket. Brittany watched the whole time, a smile on her face. And then the smile grew broader as she reached over and pulled a can off a shelf. "You're going to need air freshener!" she squealed. Andi was confused . . . until Brittany pressed down on the top of the can, sending a spray of string flying into the air.

"What do you think?" Bex asked when the string stopped spraying and they stood there, covered in strands of pink.

Andi sighed. "I *think* it's going to make a big mess," she answered honestly. Messes and the Mack house did *not* go together.

Bex nodded in agreement. Then she turned to Brittany. "We'll take twenty." Putting on a pair of over-sized black shades, she waggled her eyebrows at Andi.

There was nothing Andi could do but roll her eyes back at Bex. She had protested as much as she could protest. She had warned Bex as much as she could warn her. It didn't seem to matter. Bex was determined to make the most out of their freedom. They were having a party—even if it was probably the worst idea in the history of ideas.

* * *

The rest of the afternoon went by fast. Too fast, in Andi's opinion. She would have liked some more time to wrap her head around throwing her first official party, but between shopping for party snacks, decorating, and buying the perfect outfit, it was party time before she knew it.

Running upstairs, she stared down at the dress laid out on her bed. It was perfect. Just looking at it made her smile. It was a gorgeous yellow, with a pleated front that made the short skirt billow out right above her knees. She had added handmade bows to the shoulders and found a slim silver headband with four yellow flowers on it to match. When she had seen the dress on the rack, she had known she had to have it. But now, looking at it on her bed, Andi's stomach flipped nervously. It was one thing to wear it in her room. It was an entirely different thing to wear it in front of a room full of people at her first party.

Taking a deep breath, she put it on. There was no use overthinking it now. She looked at the clock on her bedside table. People were going to be arriving any minute. Checking her reflection one last time in the full-length mirror, she ran her hands over the yellow skirt and headed downstairs.

As she made her way down, she heard Bex humming to herself. Pausing midway down the stairs, she looked out over the living room. It had been transformed. A glittering ball swung from the ceiling, catching the dimmed lighting and making the whole room sparkle.

Bex had strung pixie lights across the ceiling and over the fireplace mantel, adding to the chill vibe. Balloons hung from various pictures on the walls and lined the corners of the room. There were bowls of snacks and party favors spread out, and Bex had set up a DJ table in the middle.

It looked amazing. And for the first time that day, Andi allowed herself to get a little excited.

Hearing Andi's footsteps, Bex ran over. Her eyes shone with emotion as she watched Andi come the rest of the way down the stairs. Mistaking the look for disapproval, Andi nervously fiddled with the skirt of her dress. "Do I look okay?" she asked.

"You look okay," Bex said, straight-faced. Andi's heart dropped. But then a huge smile spread across Bex's face, and she let out a squeal. "You look *amazing*!" she cried.

Relief flooded Andi. "So do you!" she said. And it was true. Bex had put braids in the front of her hair and was wearing a flowing cardigan over a white crocheted top. She looked like she was ready to go to an amazing concert, not a middle school party.

Just then, the doorbell rang. "Our first guests have

arrived!" Bex said, giving Andi an excited look. "Door's open!"

A moment later, the door swung open, revealing Buffy and Cyrus. Their eyes grew wide. When Andi had told them she was having a party, both of her friends had been surprised. Andi was not one for breaking the rules. And she was definitely not one to throw a party. But as they looked around the transformed living room, it was clear to them that Andi was changing.

"We aren't the first ones here, are we?" Buffy asked after they had given their approval. At Andi's nod, she let out a huge groan. "We are *soooo* lame! Who else is coming?"

"Everybody who saw my post," Andi answered quickly. *Although,* she added silently, *I didn't post* that *long ago. Maybe no one saw it?* Maybe no one would come? Maybe her first party would be a total dud? But then, just before her brain exploded, Cyrus piped up.

"Oh, and I told my mom," he said.

Andi looked over at Bex. A slow smile spread over her face. If Cyrus had told his mom, they weren't going to have to worry about people coming.

CHAPTER 4

Andi's party was rocking. Apparently, her invitation—or Cyrus's mom's talent for gossip—had come through, and her house was full of people. Music was blaring from the speakers as Bex spun her tunes, and kids were dancing and laughing and having a blast.

Looking around, Andi couldn't believe it. She was throwing a party. She was throwing a *good* party. Granted, she didn't know half the people who were there, and she was pretty sure someone had spilled juice on Celia's favorite rug, but she didn't care. Not too much, at least. It was totally worth it. And it was still early!

As Bex led the partygoers in a chant of "Go, Andi!" Andi made her way through the dancers toward the front door. She figured, as hostess, she should probably greet people as they arrived. Just as she got to the door, it opened, revealing Jonah Beck. Her heart began to pound in a way that was becoming far too familiar. She had begun to think of it as the Beck Beat.

"This is a great party," he said, looking around at all the people.

Andi smiled nervously. "It's my first one," she said, hoping the loud music was drowning out her pounding heart. Jonah was, much to her disappointment, dating a high school girl. He probably went to parties all the time. He certainly looked comfortable in the middle of the chaos.

"I see you over there, Jonah Beck!"

Andi's head whipped around at the sound of Bex's voice. Ever since her unfortunate discovery of Andi's not-so-small crush on Jonah, Bex had been doing things to "help" her get closer to him. That included the surprise Frisbee lesson that had resulted in Andi agreeing to try out for the Ultimate Frisbee team, and now it appeared it was also going to include forcing them to dance.

Luckily, Jonah did not seem bothered by the

attention. When Bex shouted for him to show everyone his moves, to Andi's surprise, he did just that. Swinging his arms and kicking his feet, he moved to the beat of the song with surprising rhythm—and a little swagger. Andi couldn't help laughing, and she couldn't help saying yes when he asked her to dance, either.

There were many things that made Andi self-conscious: Playing Frisbee. Sports in general. Getting called on in class. Talking to Jonah. But one thing that she was oddly *not* self-conscious about was dancing. Maybe it was the fun moves Bex would show her whenever she would visit. Whatever the reason, she loved dancing. And now, as she and Jonah moved to the music, she had to admit that dancing with *him* was even better.

As the music grew louder, Andi felt the rest of the crowd fade away. It was as if she and Jonah were in their own little bubble. Together, they jumped up and down to the increasing beat, lifting their hands in the air and moving around each other as if they had done this a thousand times before. Andi's smile grew and grew. She didn't care that she and Jonah were taking up most of the dance floor. She didn't care that people were watching. There was nothing that could ruin this moment.

* ★ *

Across the room, Buffy was not letting anything get in the way of her moment, either. Although, in her case, the moment was between her and the sweet snacks Andi and Bex had laid out on the dining room table. Torn between the mini cupcakes with orange frosting and the large cupcakes with sweet cream frosting, she barely registered it when someone came up and stood next to her. Until that someone went and started talking.

"Do I know you?"

Looking over, Buffy resisted the urge to roll her eyes at the boy behind the voice. Talk about a lousy pickup line. Then she looked him up and down, taking in his bright blue plaid shirt and plate of food. "I think you would know if you knew me," she said, automatically falling into her characteristic snarky banter mode.

"What have you done that is so great that I would know you?" the boy asked.

Buffy raised an eyebrow. "What *haven't* I done?" she replied.

The boy looked thoughtful. "You haven't eaten a live frog," he finally said.

"Have you?" Buffy said, momentarily thrown off her game. He nodded yes. "Why would you eat a live frog?" she said, simultaneously grossed out and intrigued.

The boy was not backing down. It was like he enjoyed the challenge of flirting with Buffy as much as she enjoyed the challenge of flirting with him. "He mouthed off," the boy said, waggling his eyebrows.

"You never ate a frog," Buffy said, deciding their interaction had run its course.

The boy nodded. "Of course not," he agreed. "You're just making this part of the conversation very difficult."

"I'm just here for the cheese puffs," Buffy said with a shrug.

"But you're staying for the witty banter," the boy countered.

"And when does that start?" she said, shutting him down.

The boy's face fell, but he plunged on. "In a minute," he said, looking over to the corner of the dining room. "Over there. With someone else?"

Buffy had to admit it, the guy was good. He had kept her intrigued—and away from her cupcakes—for a solid two minutes. That might just be a record. And record or not, he had worked hard enough that she at least wanted to know his name. "Buffy," she said, holding out her hand.

"Marty," he said, reaching out and shaking it. Then, as if it had been his plan all along, Marty gave her a quick "check ya later" and headed back into the crowd of partygoers.

Buffy turned back to the food, a smile on her face. That had been fun. Strange and a little intense, but fun. Hearing footsteps, she turned, thinking it would be Marty, back for more banter. But it was only Cyrus. He had heard the tail end of the conversation.

"Hey," he said, catching wind of potential drama. "Who was that kid you were talking to?"

Buffy pretended to think hard for a moment. Then she shrugged. "I don't remember his name," she said, even though that was not even close to true. But when she got going on playing the "game," she had a hard time stopping—even if it meant being vague and somewhat hard to read with her best friend. "I was too busy one-upping him."

"Conversation is not a competition sport, Buffy," Cyrus said, leaning over the desserts and rolling his eyes dramatically. It wasn't the first time he had witnessed Buffy trying to "win" a conversation.

"Maybe not yet," Buffy replied. Then, unable to stop herself, she added, "But the night is young. And so am I!"

As Cyrus groaned, Buffy grabbed one more cupcake and took off into the crowd. Cyrus watched her go, simultaneously annoyed and jealous. He talked a big game, but when it came to flirting, he could probably use some tips from Buffy. But he would never admit that—at least not to her. Maybe to Andi. Speaking of Andi, he realized he hadn't checked in with the hostess of the evening in a while. Not since he had seen her rocking the dance floor with Jonah. Scanning the room, he spotted his bestie watching the crowd.

"Hey!" he said, walking over and joining her.

Hearing Cyrus's voice, Andi turned. A huge grin spread over her face. "I think people are having a good time," she said happily. "I'm throwing . . . a fun party!"

"Go you," Cyrus said, lifting his hand. The pair bumped fists.

And then, suddenly, the music shifted and the crowds parted. Turning to see what was going on, Andi felt her stomach drop. She should have known things were too good to last. Because there, dancing in the middle of the crowd, was none other than Amber— aka Jonah Beck's obnoxious but perfectly perfect high school girlfriend. She was wearing a black tank top decorated with silver beading that sparkled, and her long blond hair was whipping back and forth as she showed off dance moves Andi thought only people in music videos knew how to do. The crowd—including Jonah—was loving it. They shouted and clapped as she bent over and then snapped up, flipping her hair.

Andi groaned. "Why does she have to be here?"

"You know what?" Cyrus said, letting out his own annoyed groan. "She shouldn't be. I'm going to ask her to leave."

"You are?" Andi asked, surprised by her best friend's sudden burst of bravado.

"Yeah," he said, smoothing down his vest. Then he

stopped and stuffed his hands into his pockets, shaking his head. "No. I only talk a big game. She terrifies me."

Andi wasn't terrified of Amber. But she wasn't a big fan of the girl. And she *definitely* didn't want to talk to her. But when the music came to an end and the "Amber Show" stopped, Andi felt a wave of nausea wash over her as Amber made her way across the room—toward her. "Ugh!" Andi said, turning to Cyrus. "She's coming over. I don't want to talk to her."

But it was too late.

"Hi, Amber," Andi said through clenched teeth. Up close, Amber looked even prettier.

"Hi, Andi," Amber said back in a sickly sweet voice. She gestured to the dance floor. "Great party."

As the two girls made awkward conversation, Cyrus watched. He didn't like confrontation. And Amber *did* scare him. But he wasn't about to let her go and ruin Andi's night with her fake nice talk and insincere compliments. "I'm sorry. I have to say something," he said, interrupting them. "We don't know each other—"

"You're Cyrus, right?" Amber said, cutting him off. Cyrus's eyes grew wide. How did she know that?

Was she psychic? "Yes. No. I don't know," he stammered. "Why?"

"My friend thinks you're cute," Amber said. "She wants to meet you. I'll introduce you."

Before Cyrus could even utter an apology, Amber grabbed his arm and began dragging him away. He looked over his shoulder, mouthing *sorry* to Andi before he disappeared into the crowd.

Andi watched them go. It had been nice of Cyrus to try to defend her, but she should have known Amber would get the upper hand. She was a high schooler, after all. Still, it stung a little that Cyrus's attention had been so quickly taken. Sighing, she looked back at the party. At least people were having fun. Andi just wished she was having a little more fun herself.

CHAPTER 5

"Did you smell that? Something stinks in here."

Hearing Bex's voice, Andi turned. Crinkling her nose, she sniffed the air. She didn't smell anything. What was Bex talking about? Then she looked down, and her eyes grew wide with understanding. In her hands, Bex was holding the special cans they had bought at The Fringe.

"If only we had air freshener," Andi said, a huge grin breaking on her face. It was as if Bex had read her mind. She needed a dose of fun. And what was more fun than spraying unsuspecting party people with loads of pink sticky string?

Holding the can up in front of her, Andi pressed down. Pink string shot out and over the crowd. As some of the kids began to shriek, other kids found more of the cans and joined in the action. Soon the entire first floor of the Macks' house was a sticky string battlefield. The music blasted, and people were jumping up and down, spraying the cans to the beat as they waved their hands in the air. No one was safe. And everyone was having a blast.

Everyone, that is, except Amber.

Spotting her coming from the kitchen, Bex let loose with her own can of green spray string. She was no fool. She knew how stuck up and rude Amber had been to Andi ever since Andi had become friends with Jonah. She had seen the fake smile Amber had given Andi as the two girls talked. Bex had known girls like Amber in high school. She hadn't liked them then, and she really didn't like them now. Pressing harder on the nozzle, she emptied the entire contents of the can onto Amber's perfect blond head.

Bex walked off and left the girl fuming.

But Amber was the only one not having fun. The string war had gotten the party back in full swing. With the cans emptied, kids quickly returned to the dance floor. One after another, they showed off their signature dance moves. Bex kept the music rocking so Cyrus could shake his arms in the air and Buffy could show off a sick split. And if they weren't dancing, kids were in the selfie booth, trying on costumes and snapping pics. It was shaping up to be a night none of them would—or could—forget.

And then, suddenly, the lights went out.

The music stopped.

The whole house seemed to be put on pause. Kids stopped dancing. People stopped taking pictures. It grew silent.

And then, a slow beat began to fill the house. A black light came on, illuminating neon green and yellow paint that lined the walls and stairs. Then a lone figure appeared—or what looked like a figure. All anyone could see in the black light was a pair of bright neon green gloves and stripes of blue neon that ran up and down the center of the figure's body and onto its arms and legs. All eyes were on the figure as it bopped and weaved its way down the stairs to the music. Reaching the bottom of the stairs, the figure's bright green shoes glided over the wood in an intricate and practiced pattern. It was, hands—and feet—down, the coolest thing that had happened all night.

Finally, the music stopped, and the lights came back on.

Standing there, in a cool black tracksuit with a hood over her hair, was Andi. She smiled as the crowd, led by Jonah, began to chant her name. She had thought Bex was crazy when she suggested Andi do that, but now, hearing everyone call out her name, she was glad she had. It had pushed her completely out of her comfort zone, like when Bex had made her play Ultimate Frisbee. But, she realized now, that wasn't entirely a bad thing. Maybe she had spent too much time trying to hide, when she should have been doing things like this all along. Because it felt pretty darn great.

Amber, however, was not pleased with the response to Andi's little show. She was especially unimpressed by Jonah's enthusiastic response. Her eyes narrowed. Then she ran halfway up the stairs so that everyone could see—and hear—her.

"And let's not forget about Andi's new mom," Amber cried. Clapping her hands, she began to chant, "Bex! Bex! Bex!"

Confused by the support, but not bothered by it, Andi chanted along with everyone else. She caught Bex's eye and gave her a big smile. This night would never have happened without her. *Thank you,* she mouthed.

Then Amber went on. "And what about Andi's new dad?" she said. Her voice was insincere and her eyes cold as she pretended to look around the room. "Is *he* here? We'd love to meet him, too."

Andi's stomach dropped as she felt everyone turn and look at her. All the good feelings that had been rushing through her disappeared, replaced by icy sadness and disappointment. Her limbs felt heavy, and every beat of her heart was slow and painful. As if in slow motion, she swung her head to where Bex stood. Their eyes met. Neither needed to speak to know what the other one was thinking. Bex was mortified—for Andi. And Andi? Andi was mortified for herself.

Go! Bex mouthed, knowing the best thing for Andi to do now was escape for a bit. She punched a key on the panel in front of her, and the lights went out.

When they came back on, Andi was gone.

✱ ★ ✸

Andi had gone to the one place that always made her feel better. Andi Shack, the one-room house she and her parents—or rather, her grandparents—had decorated and made into her crafts place was the one spot she could go and feel safe. Always. The walls, lined with colorful art supplies, never judged. The soft pillow that she had decorated didn't care if she cried on it. Most important, the shack couldn't lie to her and didn't have any secrets.

Sitting on the small porch, Andi stared down at her hands. She looked at the long, thin fingers, with the slightly thicker knuckles and the one visible vein that beat now as her heart struggled to slow and her brain struggled to process what had just happened. Her dad. Who was he? Did her hands look like his? Did he like to dance? Had he ever been completely and utterly humiliated?

"Hey."

Bex's voice broke through Andi's thoughts. Looking up, she watched as Bex crossed the lawn and sat down on the porch. "Feel like some company?" Bex asked hopefully.

"No," Andi said, answering honestly. She had had

enough company for one night. For a lot of nights, actually.

Unfortunately, Bex didn't appear to hear her. Or if she did, she chose to ignore her. "That girl has no boundaries," she said. "What kind of person thinks it's okay to come out and ask an intensely personal question like that?"

For a long moment, the only sounds were the crickets chirping in the woods behind the shack and the muted beat of the music coming from inside the house. Andi *wanted* to agree with Bex. She *wanted* to be mad at Amber and think she was horrible and terrible. But Andi had to acknowledge that the only thing Amber had done was ask the same question she herself had been asking Bex for days. "Me," she finally said. "I do it to you. All the time." She paused. "Are you ever going to tell me who my dad is?"

"Of course," Bex said quickly. Instantly, Andi leaned forward, her hands clutching the sides of her chair with nervous anticipation. "Oh. Like right now?" Bex said, looking suddenly nervous herself.

"Why not?" Andi said, shrugging. "Are you planning to go back to the party? Because I'm not." She smiled, trying to lighten the mood, but her eyes were brimming with emotion. "And I don't really want any pizza."

Bex opened her mouth. For one second, Andi felt a glimmer of hope. This was it. She was going to find out who her father was. She was going to hear his name. . . .

"Bex! Andi!"

Instead, she heard Cyrus screeching *her* name. Looking over, she saw her best friend leaning out the back door. His usually carefully coiffed hair was disheveled; his vest was askew and his eyes were wide. Bex and Andi shared a look. This couldn't be good.

"Your parents are here!"

They were wrong. This was way worse than not good. This was, in fact, the end of the world.

CHAPTER 6

Andi had heard the expression "If looks could kill," but she had always thought it was an exaggeration. Until now.

Celia stood staring at Bex and Andi—or rather, glaring at them—her lips pursed. She didn't say a thing. She hadn't said a thing since chasing everyone out. She hadn't said a thing while turning off the music and taking stock of the damage. She hadn't even said anything when she'd seen the stain on her favorite rug. Her lips had just grown tighter and tighter until they formed one single, thin straight line of disappointment.

And then, just when Andi was sure Celia was never going to speak again—she exploded. There was finger-pointing and "I trusted you" and "I couldn't be more disappointed" and "I should have known!" When the screaming stopped, all Andi and Bex could do was fall back onto the couch, their hands in their laps, their heads hung in shame.

"I hope you got all that," Ham said after his wife disappeared up the stairs. Making sure they knew they had to clean—all night if necessary—he nodded and followed Celia out of the room.

"Scary," Andi said when he was gone and the coast was clear. "I've never seen her that angry."

"You know what's scarier?" Bex asked. "Neither have I."

Andi sighed. Slapping her hands on the tops of her legs, she stood up. She didn't want to risk making the woman any madder by not doing as they had been told. And they had been told to make the house spotless. Looking around the room, Andi let out an even bigger sigh. That wasn't going to be easy. The place was a complete and utter disaster. Piles of sticky string were bunched up in the corners, and long strands hung from the chandelier and floor lamps. Chips had fallen out of bowls and been crunched under dozens of feet until the crumbs were embedded in the rugs.

Somehow soda had ended up on the walls—not to mention the black light paint Celia didn't even know about yet.

Moving around the room, Andi began to pick up odds and ends. "Don't worry about it," Bex said as she, too, began to clean. "I'll make it clear that you were against this party the whole time."

"Except that's not true," Andi said, stopping and walking over to Bex. "I *want* people to think it was my party." She stopped and looked around at the mess. Then she smiled. "Because it was a great one! Thank you!"

Bex smiled back at Andi. "It was my pleasure," she said, pulling Andi in for a hug. She knew that they didn't have the traditional mother/daughter relationship. They might not ever have that kind of relationship. But she wanted to make Andi happy, no matter what. And if that meant throwing a party for her and taking the blame, or *not* taking the blame as the case might be, then that was what she would do.

As they stood there, Ham walked back into the living room. Leaning down, he picked up a decorative birdcage strung with little lights and righted it.

"Hey, Dad," Bex said. "Sorry we ruined your vacation."

"Doesn't matter," Ham said, walking over to them. "It was just the first one—in thirteen years."

"Why did you come home?" Andi asked, curious. Considering how long it had been, it seemed strange that they would cut it short.

Ham sighed. "We got a call from the neighborhood watch," he explained. "They were very concerned. They had never heard anything resembling the sound of parties coming from our house before."

Bex and Andi exchanged small, triumphant grins. While the outcome hadn't been what they were hoping for—at least not on the parental front—the party had obviously been a success. No boring party ever got shut down for excessive noise.

Choosing to ignore the look between the two girls, Ham reached out and gave Andi a squeeze on her shoulders. "Hey, why don't you go to bed?" he said gently. "I'll help Bex clean up."

Andi had to admit that bed sounded *really* good right then. She had been thinking about crawling into her big comfy bed ever since the last guest had slipped out the door. But she wasn't about to leave the two of them to clean up after her party. Unless, of course, they really wanted to do the cleaning. Turning, she looked up at Bex with a questioning expression.

"It's okay," Bex said, granting her permission. "Go."

Giving her a grateful smile and a sincere thank-you, Andi reached out and wrapped her arm around Ham. "Sorry, Pops," she said, squeezing him tightly. Even if she still wanted to know who her biological father was, it didn't mean Ham was any less her father. And his hugs still made her feel better, no matter what was going on.

With a kiss on her head from Ham, Andi turned to go. But then she stopped. There was one last thing she had to say before her head hit the pillow and she conked out. "We *are* going to have that conversation, right?" she said, giving Bex a serious look. "The one we started outside?"

Bex nodded. "Yes," she said. "I promise."

Satisfied, Andi turned and headed upstairs. Bex and her father watched the younger girl go. Silence fell over the living room as, for a long moment, neither said anything. Then Bex let out a deep sigh and resumed picking up. Watching his daughter as she collected boas and the odd cowboy hat, Ham grew thoughtful. He had seen Bex upset before, but he had never seen her like this. It was as though she were carrying a heavy weight on her shoulders and it was pushing her—and her spirit—down. He knew that his wife was still furious Bex had told Andi the truth, but he wasn't. Not really. He was proud of his daughter for taking ownership of her life. And he didn't want to see her regret that decision now.

"What's she talking about?" he asked, reaching down to pick up a pillow from the floor. "What conversation?"

"She wants to know who her father is," Bex said. "She won't stop asking." As the words left her mouth, she realized how desperately she needed advice. This whole parenting thing was so new to her. She spent every minute of every day worrying she was going to mess up Andi's life—or mess it up even more than she had by keeping the secret in the first place. Sighing, she sank back down on the couch and stared at the blue boa on her lap, fiddling with the fake feathers. "What am I supposed to tell her?" she finally said.

"The truth," her father said simply.

"I'm just not sure how many life-altering blows she can handle," Bex said. "'Hi, I'm your mom,' followed by 'Your dad doesn't even know you exist.'"

"He knows."

Bex looked over at her father. His head was down and he seemed oddly fixated on plumping the pillow in front of him. Her eyes narrowed. Then her heart began to pound as what he had said sank in. "What's that?" she repeated, hoping maybe she had just misheard him. Maybe he had said, "It snows," or "This goes."

But she hadn't misheard him. "Andi's father," he said. "He knows she exists."

Bex was shocked. Her ears rang, and she felt suddenly sick to her stomach. She had spent the past thirteen years clinging to the belief that she had kept two secrets—one from Andi, and one from Andi's father. And now it turned out he knew? She shook her head. "Who told him?" she finally asked.

Coming around the couch, Bex's father sat down next to her. He put a hand on her knee and gave it a squeeze. "I did," he said. His eyes were kind and his voice soft as he broke the news to his daughter. He hadn't wanted to tell her like this. He hadn't wanted to have to tell her at all. But he had spent too long keeping too many secrets. Now that Andi knew the truth about her mother, she deserved to know the truth about her father. Even if it was going to make things a bit bumpier for Bex.

*　*　*

Andi thought she would fall asleep the moment her head hit the pillow, but it turned out she was wrong. Long after she turned off the light and got under the covers, she lay awake, staring up at the scarves Bex had sent her that she had turned into a canopy. She listened to the muted sound of Bex and Ham talking until they finally headed to bed and the hallway light turned off. Then she lay there simply listening to the house as it settled into the night, creaking and groaning as it shifted on its foundation.

She had thrown her first party. And not only had she thrown her first party, she had thrown her first party and it had been awesome. Images from the night kept flashing through her mind. Dancing with Jonah, showering people with strands of pink string, her stairway entrance. She saw Buffy and Cyrus having a blast, and she saw Bex in the middle of it all, guiding the night like a ship's captain.

When she had found out Bex was her mother, not her sister, Andi had been convinced her life was never going to be the same. And it turned out it wasn't. It wasn't the same at all. Because now she had someone in her life who wanted her to stand out and stand up for herself. She had someone who wanted her to dare to live life to the fullest. And while that meant she might get in a *little* bit of trouble, it also meant she was going to have so much fun.

She sighed, turning over and snuggling farther down under her covers. Now, she thought as sleep finally found her, if she could just find out who her father was and why Bex was so determined to keep him a secret. She yawned. But Bex *had* promised to tell her. So she would just wait and see. For now, she would go to sleep, visions of her party dancing in her head.